THE PUMPKIN PATCH

A Traditional Buddhist Tale

HEIAN

Text copyright   © 2004 Sybil Taylor

Illustrations copyright © 2004 June Atkin

Originally published Hard Cover Edition as
"The Pumpkin Patch" ISBN: 0-89346-935-1

First Paper Back Edition 2004
04 05 06 07 08 09 10 9 8 7 6 5 4 3 2 1

Heian International Inc.
20655 S. Western Ave., Suite 105
Torrance, CA 90501

Web site: www. heian.com
E-mail: heianemail@earthlink.net

ISBN: 0-89346-942-4

THE PUMPKIN PATCH

A Traditional Buddhist Tale

Retold by
SYBIL TAYLOR

Illustrated by
JUNE ATKIN

HEIAN

There was once a very wise old man
who lived in the country in a little house
with a garden where he grew good things to eat.

The old man loved
all the living things around him

and especially . . .

He liked to watch
his pumpkin patch grow...

But one day the pumpkins began to quarrel . . .

"I'm the biggest one."

"So what, you're crowding me."

"I'm the sweetest."

"I'm the highest to the sky."

"I'm the roundest."

"You're mean."

"I don't care,
you're just a baby."

"I'm the closest to the earth."

When the old man heard all the racket he looked out of his window and said, "Please, pumpkins, stop."

12

"Shhhhhh - no more talking. Just sit very, very quietly together.
Sit very, very still and very, very silent.

Like this . . .”

"Why?" asked the littlest pumpkin.

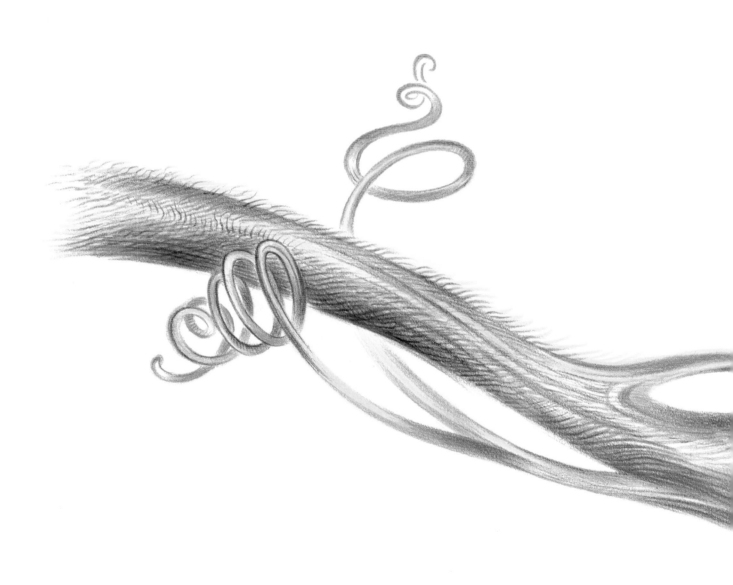

But the wise old man just smiled and said,

"Try it and see."

The sun went down over the garden
and in the pumpkin patch
the pumpkins sat very, very still
and very, very silent . . .
stars and moon came out and
the old man slept and . . .

The pumpkins continued to sit very, very still
and very, very silent. Rain fell and clouds flew by,
and still the pumpkins sat on, until, at last . . .
the morning sun rose up.

"Pumpkins," the old man said, "did you learn something?"

"Yes," they all said happily.
We learned that
we all feel the same things.
We all feel the warm sun on our skins
helping us to be strong and to grow."

"We all feel the raindrops
bringing fresh water to the earth
and to the thirsty roots
of our vine mother.
We all feel our vine mother
drinking up the water and feeding it
to each and every one of us through our stems."

"And we know that one . . .

and all . . .

all and one . . .

we are connected together

in a single . . .

great . . .

big . . .

beautiful . . .

pumpkin patch."

And the wise old man smiled and said, "Good,"
and then he went into his house and ate a delicious breakfast.

THE BUDDHA WAY

Remember the last time you were upset and angry? Maybe it was when you were arguing with someone in your family. Or maybe, like the pumpkins in this story, you quarreled with your friends. You probably felt unhappy and maybe even lonely because nobody seemed to understand.

In this story too, when the pumpkins in the pumpkin patch are quarreling they are not happy. They are so upset that they cannot listen to each other without being angry. They are so busy being mad, they forget to look around at all the things going on in the world around them – things like a bug taking a walk on a leaf, or a cloud changing shape in the sky, or a sad friend who needs cheering up.

Luckily, the wise old man in the story knew a way to help the pumpkins, a way discovered long ago in India by a great teacher named Sakyamuni Buddha. Although you are not a pumpkin, Buddha's way can help you too when you are feeling mad, sad, lonely, afraid or mean.

Remember in the story, how the pumpkins stopped quarreling when they sat very quietly? Sitting like this is part of Buddha's way, and it is called meditation. First, you pick a quiet place. Then, you sit up straight but comfortably. Next, look down with your eyes not quite closed and just breathe in and breathe out, very softly and very smoothly, through your nose. Sit quietly like that for a while and feel how gently the air of your breath moves into your body and then moves out again.

Sometimes, when you are sitting like that, you start thinking about things. Maybe you think about things like how you are still mad or about how you are hungry or want to go out and play. That is okay, everybody thinks of things all the time. All you do when that happens is feel your breath again – how it moves in and out of your body – in and out.

Most of the time, doing this will make you feel really still and calm, just the way a glass of water gets when you stop stirring it. Meditation helps people to be peaceful like the pumpkins were after they sat quietly in the rain and sun. Sitting quietly, they felt the warm rays of the sun and the pit-pat of raindrops on their leaves, and they did not feel like shouting at each other any more. Sitting quietly, they were able to notice that all of them were growing from the same vine.

Like the pumpkins all together on their vine, we are all here together in the world – fishes, birds, butterflies, snakes, cats, dogs, giraffes, tigers, trees, flowers, the big rivers, oceans, the sun, the moon, the stars and you and me. We are like pieces in a huge puzzle all fitting together to make one big picture. Every creature, every spider, every lion, every boy and every girl – and you and me too – are like the pieces. We all have a special place in the world and without every one of us, the puzzle would not be complete.

Buddha taught people how to meditate. He helped people see that because we all fit together to make the big world puzzle, each of us is important. He saw that all beings want to be happy, and he tried to help. He thought everyone could help. Maybe you would like to try Buddha's way and see for yourself?

SUGGESTED DISCUSSION QUESTIONS

1. Can you remember the last time you were angry or upset ?

2. How did you feel when you were angry or upset ?

3. How do you feel when a grown-up wants you to do something you do not like ?

4. What do you do to feel better when you are upset ?

5. Do you like everyone better when you are happy ?

6. How do you feel inside when you sit quietly ?

7. How does your body feel when you sit quietly ?

8. What do you hear when you sit quietly ?

9. If you sit quietly when you are already happy, how does it feel ?

10. What do you think would happen if you meditated a few minutes each day ?

11. When you meditate with your mother, father, family or friends does it feel different ?

12. The pumpkins learned something: do you think you learned something from this story too ?